WALT DISNEY'S
BRER RABBIT
Gets Tricked

Random House 🏠 New York

One day Brer Rabbit took a walk.
He sang and danced down the path.
Then he smelled some flowers.
Brer Turtle watched him do all this.

"You look silly!" said Brer Turtle.

Brer Rabbit laughed and said, "If you were as smart as I am, you would sing and dance, too."

Humpf! thought Brer Turtle.
He thinks he is so smart!
I will teach him a lesson.

So Brer Turtle said,
"You may be smart. But I
am the fastest creature in
the world!"

Brer Rabbit laughed.

"You, fast?" he said.
"You bet," said Brer Turtle.
They agreed to race the next day.

They would start at the big tree.
They would finish at the old well.
There were two ways to go.
"I'll take the high road," said Brer Rabbit.
"I'll take the low road," said Brer Turtle.

Brer Turtle could not run fast.
But he had a plan to trick Brer Rabbit.
That night he told his family all about it.

Early the next morning, Brer Turtle
and his family crept into the woods.

Mrs. Turtle went over to the big tree.

Soon it was time for the race to begin.
Brer Turtle was hiding at the finish line.
The children hid at the crossroads.
Mrs. Turtle was at the starting line.
She looked just like Brer Turtle!

"On your mark, get set, go!"
said Brer Buzzard.

The two racers were off!

Brer Rabbit ran as fast as he could.

Suddenly one of the turtle children
ran across the road.

Brer Rabbit thought it was Brer Turtle!

"He is ahead of me!" said Brer Rabbit.
"How did that happen?"

Brer Rabbit ran faster.

But at each crossroad, there
was a turtle ahead of him.

Just as Brer Rabbit came to the finish
line, he saw Brer Turtle cross it first.

Everyone cheered Brer Turtle.

Brer Rabbit went home.
His ears were drooping.

If I'm not fast anymore,
maybe I'm not smart either,
he thought sadly.

Brer Rabbit was so sad that
he went right to bed.

"Brer Fox, Brer Wolf, Brer Bear—
they would love to catch a dumb
rabbit like me," he said.

Mrs. Rabbit said, "Go ask Aunt
Mammy-Bammy, the wise rabbit,
for help."

So Brer Rabbit started off.

Aunt Mammy-Bammy
lived in a swamp.
To get there, Brer
Rabbit had to crawl . . .

swim . . .

jump . . .

slide . . .

climb . . .

and wade.
Finally he got there.

"Aunt Mammy-Bammy!" called Brer Rabbit.
"I need your help."

"Why?" Aunt Mammy-Bammy asked.
"What is wrong?"

"I'm not smart anymore!" said Brer Rabbit.
Then the wise Mammy-Bammy said, "Bring
me fruit from the zitzat tree. Then I'll try
to help you."

Brer Rabbit set off.
Suddenly Brer Wolf grabbed him!

Brer Wolf took Brer Rabbit to his house.

"At last I caught you," he said.

"I am smarter than you are!"

He tied Brer Rabbit up.

Brer Rabbit had an idea.

He sang a song.

"That's a nice song," said Brer Wolf.

"There is a dance to go with it,"
Brer Rabbit told him.

"Show it to me," Brer Wolf said.

"The rope is in my way!" cried Brer Rabbit.

So Brer Wolf untied the rope.
And Brer Rabbit danced right out the door!

Then he ran smack into Brer Bear.

Brer Bear caught him with his big paw.
"Why are you running?" growled Brer Bear.

Suddenly Brer Rabbit had another idea.
"I'm running after the money machine!" he said.
"What is a money machine?" asked Brer Bear.

"It looks like a wagon. When the back
wheels catch up to the front wheels,
gold coins fly!" said Brer Rabbit.

Just then a wagon came down the road.

"There it is!" cried Brer Rabbit.
"How do I get the money?"
hollered Brer Bear.
"Run behind it!" said Brer Rabbit.
"And keep your eyes on the wheels!"

Brer Bear ran after the wagon
to catch the gold coins.

Brer Rabbit ran to find the zitzat tree.
He went into the thickest part of the woods.

Suddenly Brer Fox sprang out.
"At last I've got you!" he said.

Brer Rabbit looked up at the pine cones.
Aha! he thought. I know how to escape!

"What are you looking at?" asked Brer Fox.
"The plums on this tree," Brer Rabbit
said. "They are the sweetest plums you
have ever tasted!"

"How do I get one?" asked Brer Fox.

"Lie under the tree until one drops,"
Brer Rabbit told him.

"When will it drop?" asked Brer Fox.

"Any minute!" called Brer Rabbit.
And away he hopped.

Brer Rabbit went back to the swamp.

"Aunt Mammy-Bammy," said Brer Rabbit.

"I had no time to find the zitzat tree!"

"Why not? Why not?" asked the wise rabbit.

Brer Rabbit told how he
escaped from Brer Wolf . . .

and Brer Bear . . .

and Brer Fox.

"But I didn't do what you asked me.
Now I will never be smart again!"
said Brer Rabbit.

The wise rabbit laughed and said,
"If you were any smarter, I would
have to give you my job!"

Brer Rabbit hopped all the way home.
Soon he was singing and dancing again.
"I am the smartest creature of all!"
he sang happily.
But Brer Turtle knew better.